A Second Look

Jennie Abbott

W9-DDP-095

Fearon
Belmont, California

DOUBLE FASTBACK® ROMANCE Books

Chance of a Lifetime
Follow Your Dream
Good-Bye and Hello
Kiss and Make Up
Love in Bloom
A Love to Share
Never Too Late
No Secrets
The Road to Love
A Second Look

Cover illustrator: Terry Hoff

ISBN 0-8224-2385-5
Library of Congress Catalog Card Number: 86-81659
Printed in the United States of America
1. 9 8 7 6 5 4 3 2

"This is definitely the worst movie I've ever seen," thought Lisa. Then she added, "But what a great night!"

Lisa Munroe was sitting in a darkened movie theater. Rick's arm was around her shoulders, and Lisa was completely happy. The movie, though, was terrible. It was called *Night of Terror.* Lisa hated horror movies, but she wasn't really paying attention, anyway. Being out with Rick was so exciting that she couldn't concentrate on anything else. She kept her eyes on the screen while she relived the events of the last few weeks.

Lisa had first met Rick Tobin when he had come into Van's Video just after New Year's, about a month ago. Lisa was the store's assistant manager. From the moment Rick had first walked into Van's, Lisa had been dying to go out with him. Since they'd met, he had come in at least twice a week to rent or return tapes. But they'd never seemed to get any further than a friendly chat.

Lisa thought back to all the plans she had devised to capture Rick's interest. She smiled to herself, remembering the tapes she had reserved for him. Reserving tapes for customers was strictly against Van's policy. Van, Lisa's boss, said rentals were to be strictly on a first-come-first-served basis.

Then there had been the times when Lisa had hung around the record store where Rick worked. The store was just down the street from Van's, so Lisa had gone there sometimes on her lunch breaks. None of her efforts had paid off, though. Rick had always been friendly, but he hadn't asked her out.

By yesterday afternoon, Lisa had just about given up hope. But then Rick had come into Van's and headed right for her. She had practically memorized the ensuing conversation, word for word.

"Hi," Lisa had said. "Can I help you?" Her heart had been pounding.

"That depends on what you mean," Rick had replied, smiling into Lisa's eyes.

"Is there a special tape you're looking for?" Lisa had continued. She had felt herself blushing as Rick continued to smile.

"Nope," he said. "I just came in to ask you a question."

"OK, shoot," Lisa had said as casually as possible.

Then Rick had spoken the words Lisa wanted to hear. "What are you doing Saturday night?"

"I'm free Saturday," Lisa had answered, trying not to sound too enthusiastic.

"Just wondering," Rick had said with a shrug. Then he'd pretended to walk toward the door.

There had been a horrible second before Lisa realized he was joking. Then he had turned back to her and said, "Just kidding. Would you like to go to a movie?" There had been the most adorable, crooked grin on his face.

"Sure," Lisa had said, completely forgetting her "cool" act. "I'd love to."

And tonight, here she was with Rick.

Lisa's thoughts and the movie ended at the same time. Lisa wasn't sorry the movie was over, but she was sorry that Rick had to take his arm off her shoulder.

"How'd you like the movie?" he asked as they left the theater.

"I loved it," Lisa answered. Then she thought, "That's not really a lie. I hated the movie, but I loved sitting next to him."

Rick held her hand as they walked back to her apartment. As they got closer to her building, Lisa began to wonder when she would see him again. Would he say anything about another date? Should she say something if he didn't?

Finally, they were standing in front of Lisa's door. Rick put both his hands on her shoulders and smiled that wonderful smile at her. Then he pulled her toward him and gave her a long, long kiss. "I've wanted to do that all night," he whispered.

Lisa didn't know how long they stood with their arms around each other. Finally, Rick held her away from him, smiled again, tousled her curly blond hair, and was gone.

At first, Lisa just stood in the hallway, wide-eyed and breathless. She stared at the corner around which

Rick had just disappeared. Then, her heart still racing, she leaned back against her apartment door and closed her eyes. She hugged herself, imagining that Rick was still holding her. She relived that long, romantic kiss. Finally, she opened her eyes and took a moment to come back to reality. She knew that her roommate Ginny would be inside waiting to hear about her date.

As Lisa fished in her purse for her keys, some disturbing thoughts entered her mind. Rick hadn't asked her for another date. He hadn't even said he'd had a good time, or that he *wanted* to see her again. In fact, he hadn't said much of anything.

Suddenly, Lisa couldn't wait to get inside her apartment and talk to Ginny about all this. Ginny was such a wonderful friend, and always so sensible.

When Lisa opened the door, she saw Ginny lying on the couch watching television. Ginny jumped up to turn off the TV and then went back to sit on the couch.

"Well, how was it?" Ginny asked excitedly. Then she noticed the expression on Lisa's face. "You look weird," Ginny said. "Did anything go wrong?"

"I'm not really sure," Lisa replied. She took off her jacket and sat down in a big armchair. Then she tucked her feet under her. "Everything started out great," she said. "Rick looked adorable. He was wearing jeans and a blue sweater that matched his eyes exactly. I adore those blue eyes of his. And that black hair makes his eyes look even bluer." She paused for a minute, picturing Rick, and then went on.

"Anyway, we got to the theater . . ."

"What did you see?" interrupted Ginny.

Lisa hesitated. Ginny knew how much she hated horror movies. *"Night of Terror,"* she mumbled. "But I didn't care, really."

"Didn't he ask you what you wanted to see?" Ginny asked.

"Well, no," answered Lisa. "Not exactly. I could have said I wanted to see something else, I guess. But who was concentrating on the movie, anyway? I don't even know what it was about!"

Ginny grinned. "Well, that's probably lucky for you," she said. "But go on."

"Well, that's about it," Lisa said. "I guess there really isn't much more to tell. Rick kept his arm around me in the movie, and that was great. I just loved being near him. I felt so special sitting there!"

"So, what's the problem?" Ginny asked.

"Well, he was really quiet on the way home," Lisa said. "Then when we got up to the door, he kissed me."

"Is that all?" Ginny asked. She was still waiting for the important part of the story.

"I know this sounds silly," Lisa said, "but it wasn't an ordinary kiss. It was so romantic! We were holding each other for the longest time. And then he just walked away."

"He didn't say anything at all?" Ginny asked. "Not even, 'See you around'?" Her expression told Lisa that Ginny was beginning to wonder about Rick.

Lisa sighed. "Oh, he did say that he'd been wanting to kiss me," she said.

Ginny threw her hands in the air. "So what *is* the problem?" she asked, sounding exasperated.

"Well," Lisa said slowly, "I was hoping he'd say something about wanting to see me again. But he sort of—well—disappeared."

Then Lisa stood up and began to pace around the room. "Oh, Ginny," she said. "I don't know what to think. What do *you* think of all this? Do you think he'll ask me out again?"

Ginny thought for a minute. Then she said, "Well, it all sounds a little odd to me. If I had to guess, though, I'd say that you'll probably hear from him again. But Lisa, what's so great about this guy, anyway? First, he doesn't even ask you what movie you want to see. Then he hardly talks to you all night. And to top all that off, he walks away without even saying good night!"

"That's all true," Lisa said anxiously. "But what about when he said he'd been wanting to kiss me?"

Ginny made a dismissive gesture with her hand. "That was nice," she said. "But after that, he definitely should have said good night. Or told you that he'd had a good time. Or *something*. He doesn't sound like a perfect dream. And I wonder what his taste in movies says about his brain!"

Lisa stood there, looking hopelessly at her roommate. Then Ginny suddenly snapped her fingers.

"Oh, I almost forgot to tell you that Tom called," she said. "He wants you to call him back tonight, even if it's late."

"I guess I'd better call him now," Lisa said miserably.

It seemed to Lisa that she had known Tom Hoffman forever. They had gone to grade school together, and had dated for a while in high school. But then they had just become best friends. They enjoyed the same things, liked the same music, and seemed to understand one another's feelings perfectly. They talked on the phone almost every night.

When Lisa called Tom, he asked if she wanted to go ice-skating the following Friday night. Lisa knew she'd have fun with Tom, but what if Rick asked her out for Friday? She didn't want to have to turn down a date with him. So Lisa told Tom that she was busy Friday night. The tone of Tom's reply made Lisa feel pretty awful.

"Oh, OK," Tom said disappointedly. "Maybe we can get together another night."

When Lisa hung up the phone, Ginny looked over at her. "You know," Ginny said, "Tom is really a great guy. If I weren't in love with Peter, *I'd* be interested in Tom. Why don't *you* give him a chance, Lisa?"

"Tom?" Lisa asked with surprise. "Oh, he and I aren't interested in each other that way. We're just friends. We've known each other too long, I guess."

Ginny disagreed. "I don't think Tom sees it that way," she said.

Lisa looked puzzled. "What makes you say that?" she asked.

"Oh, just the fact that he calls you nearly every night," Ginny replied. "And he stops to see you at work every chance he gets. And let's not forget the way he looks at you."

"The way he *looks* at me?" Lisa asked.

"Of course," Ginny answered. "The guy can't takes his eyes off you."

"Oh, Ginny," Lisa said playfully as she headed toward her room. "Ever since you and Peter got engaged, you've had romance on the brain."

"If I were you," Ginny called after her, "I'd take a second look at Tom. Before it's too late, that is."

"You're impossible," Lisa replied. "I'm going to sleep. See you in the morning."

$$B$$y Thursday afternoon, Lisa was really miserable. She had spent every night since Saturday the same way—watching television. But she hadn't paid attention to a single show. Each time the phone rang, she nearly jumped out of her skin. In the few seconds it took to answer, she'd say, "Please be Rick!" over and over again. But so far, he hadn't called.

Lisa had begun to view the phone as her personal enemy. And it was all the more exasperating because it rang a lot.

Ginny's boyfriend Peter called often. Lisa's friend Judy called. A man called to sell magazine subscriptions. Lisa's mother called to tell Lisa good-bye. She and Lisa's father were leaving Friday for a week in the mountains. And Tom called every night, as usual. Lisa found herself being almost rude, finding excuses to get off the phone as quickly as possible. She didn't want the line to be busy if Rick tried to call.

He had come into Van's twice that week. Lisa had tried to act casual, but without success. The first time he'd come in, she'd been so nervous that she'd given him the wrong videotape. Instead of *Back from the Dead*, she'd handed him *Back to Paris*. The second time he'd been there, she hadn't been able to find her pen. To her chagrin, Rick pointed out that it was sticking out of her shirt pocket. Both times, Rick had been friendly. Lisa, though, was finding that magical kiss of just a few nights ago hard to believe.

Ginny was no help, either. As the week wore on, she grew to dislike Rick more and more. Lisa knew that this was just Ginny's way of being loyal. She wasn't about to like anyone who made Lisa unhappy. So the more Lisa moped around waiting for the phone to ring, the more remarks Ginny made about Rick. Her comments were usually something like, "Maybe he watched too many movies about zombies and turned into one!" or "They probably don't have phones on his planet."

This afternoon was slow at the video store, so Lisa had plenty of time to brood about Rick. For the millionth time, she was trying to figure out whether she would ever hear from him again. She thought about calling him, but rejected the idea immediately. Instead, she decided to stop by the record store after work. She would leave right at five o'clock so she'd get to the store just before it closed. If she was lucky, Rick wouldn't be busy. She might even buy a record!

Yes, that's exactly what she'd do. She would ask Rick to recommend an album by Lowlife, a group she knew he liked. If Rick didn't ask her out by the time she left the store, Lisa promised herself that she'd give up on him.

Now that Lisa had a plan, she felt better. She was so intent on mentally rehearsing her conversation with Rick that she didn't notice the door to the video store open. She didn't even notice Tom standing in front of her until he said, "Hi, Lisa. A penny for your thoughts?"

Startled, Lisa said, "Oh! Hi, Tom. I . . . I was just thinking about something I have to do after work."

Then Lisa glanced at the clock on the wall. It was ten minutes to five. If she wanted to fix her hair and makeup before she left, she had better do it soon.

"Too bad," said Tom. "I stopped by to see if you wanted to go out for pizza."

Seeing Tom's open, friendly smile, Lisa remembered what Ginny had said: "If I were you, I'd take a second look at Tom." Lisa had to admit that Ginny had a point. Tom was sweet, fun to be with, and handsome. But she couldn't get Rick off her mind. There was something so romantic and mysterious about him!

"Thanks, but I can't," she replied to Tom with a smile.

"Got a date?" Tom asked.

Lisa hesitated. "Not exactly," she answered. "Listen, Tom. Can I talk to you later? I'm in a bit of a rush."

"Sure," said Tom. "Sorry to keep you. I'll call you tonight."

Before Tom was out the door, Lisa was on her way to the restroom in the back of the store. She ran a brush through her hair, touched up her makeup, and left the shop. As the door began to close behind her, she called a hurried "Bye" to Van.

Once out on the street, Lisa forced herself to walk at a normal pace. She didn't want to look as if she'd been running when she reached the record store.

Inside the store, Lisa tried not to be too obvious about looking for Rick. She flipped half-heartedly through some records, glancing around the store every few seconds. Finally, she spotted Rick. He was talking to a customer who seemed about to leave. Lisa moved down the aisle to be closer to where they were standing. In a moment, the customer headed for the door and Rick was free.

"This is it!" Lisa said to herself.

Rick still hadn't seen her. As he started to pass near her, she called, "Hi, Rick!"

Rick looked over at her. "Well, look who's here!" he said. "Are you just visiting, or can I help you with something?"

Lisa felt thoroughly unnerved in Rick's presence. But she was determined to go ahead with her plan. "Do you have anything by Lowlife?" she asked.

"Yeah, plenty," Rick answered. "I didn't know you liked their records. What do you have already?"

The truth was, Lisa couldn't stand Lowlife. They were too loud and hostile for her. She thought they sounded as if they were declaring war on their fans. "I don't have any of their albums," she said. "But I've heard them a lot on the radio. I thought you could recommend a good album."

"Well, their first release was just called *Lowlife*," Rick offered. "You could start with that. But their latest one is really great."

He flipped through the "L" section of albums and found the one he wanted. "Here it is!" he called.

Rick held up a record called *Feelin' Mean*. On the cover was a picture of four people dressed entirely in ragged black clothes. Their hair looked as if it had been styled by Dr. Frankenstein. They all appeared to be sneering directly at Lisa.

"What will Ginny say when I bring *this* home?" Lisa wondered. But she didn't care. So far, everything was going just as she'd planned. "I'll take it," she told Rick.

"Good choice," he replied. "You can pay at the cash register."

"Thanks a lot," Lisa said with a smile. "I'd better hurry. You must be about to close."

"Yeah, we are," Rick answered. "Want to walk me to the bus stop?"

"Sure," Lisa said casually. To herself, she said, "This might still work!"

Standing with Rick in the bus shelter, Lisa prayed that he would ask her what she was hoping to hear.

"I really had a nice time Saturday night," she said to him.

"So did I," Rick answered. "In fact, I've been meaning to ask you if you're free tomorrow night. I'm going bowling with some friends. Would you like to come?"

Lisa's heart skipped a beat. "Yes, I'd like to," she said.

Rick smiled and then looked over Lisa's shoulder. "Here comes my bus," he said. "I'm borrowing a car from a friend tomorrow night. I'll pick you up at eight."

"Great," Lisa said, smiling back at Rick. The bus pulled up, and Rick stepped over to it. As he started up the steps, Lisa called, "And thanks for helping me with the record!" Rick just waved in response.

Lisa watched the bus disappear. Then she walked home, clutching her record as if it were a trophy.

"What did you buy?" asked Ginny as Lisa walked into the apartment. Lisa had hoped that Ginny wouldn't notice the record.

"Just a record," Lisa answered.

"Let's see," said Ginny.

Lisa reluctantly handed over the record.

"I thought you hated Lowlife!" said Ginny. Then she stared at the cover for a moment. "Boy, they sure are ugly," she said. "Why on earth did you buy this?"

"I'll tell you," said Lisa slowly, "if you promise not to make fun of me."

"OK," said Ginny, "but first let me guess. Could this possibly have something to do with Rick?"

"As a matter of fact, it does," admitted Lisa sheepishly. "Oh, Ginny, I'm so excited! I still can't believe what happened. I went to the record store where Rick works and bought this record. Then Rick asked me to walk with him to the bus stop. That's when he asked me to go bowling with him and some friends tomorrow night."

"That's great!" Ginny said. "But . . ." Before Ginny had a chance to comment on how much Lisa hated bowling, the phone rang.

Ginny answered it. "It's Tom," she called to Lisa. Then, covering the mouthpiece, she whispered, *"Please* be nice to him."

Lisa took the phone. "Hi, Tom," she said.

"So. Did you finish your very important errand after work?" asked Tom.

Lisa was surprised to hear what she thought was a note of sarcasm in Tom's voice. Ordinarily, she would have confided in him. But tonight, something in his voice made her say just, "Yes, I did." And anyway, she couldn't really tell him about her ploy to trap Rick into asking her out. She tried to change the subject by asking Tom how his work was going, but he continued as if he hadn't heard.

"I haven't seen much of you lately," he said. "I've been hoping we could get together before I go away on Saturday."

"Where are you going?" asked Lisa with surprise.

"You know I'm going to visit my brother in Florida," replied Tom. "I'm sure I told you that. I'll be gone for two weeks."

Lisa suddenly felt terrible. Yes, Tom had told her about his vacation, but she had completely forgotten about it. "Of course, Tom," she said a little feebly. "You told me about it. I'd just forgotten. I'm sorry. Oh! And I'm busy tomorrow night." She tried not to sound too guilty. "Well, have a wonderful time!"

"Thanks," said Tom with a sigh. "I'll call you when I get back."

As she hung up the phone, Lisa thought about Tom. "He really is a special kind of guy," she said to herself. "Maybe Ginny is right. Maybe I *should* try to think of Tom as more than a best friend. But I wish I could feel the same excitement when I'm with him that I feel when I'm with Rick."

Then Lisa dismissed those thoughts. She could think about Tom later. Right now, all she wanted to think about was Friday night.

Lisa had to work until seven Friday night, so she knew she would have to rush home after work to get ready

for her date. In spite of the customers'
coming and going, the day seemed to last
forever. Lisa kept getting more and more
nervous every time she thought about a
night of bowling with Rick and his friends.
The mental image of herself dropping a
bowling ball on her foot just wouldn't go
away. And she wondered what Rick's
friends would be like. Would she like them?
Would they like her? Would she make a
complete fool of herself in front of them?
When the evening was over, would it take
more plotting to get to see Rick again?

Finally, she gave herself an order. "Just
stop thinking about it, or you won't have
any fun at all." It didn't help much, but
she did make it to seven o'clock.

When she let herself into her apartment,
Lisa was relieved to see that Ginny had
already gone out with Peter. She wasn't in

the mood to hear any more comments about Rick. And she certainly didn't want to be reminded of how much she hated bowling.

She put on her favorite jeans with a white shirt and a big blue sweater. But the sweater didn't look right, so she changed to a pink one. That one didn't look right, either, so she slipped a soft red one over her head. She liked it, but decided it would look better without the shirt under it. Finally, after she had brushed her hair and checked the mirror for total effect, she was satisfied.

While she waited for Rick, Lisa listened to her new Lowlife album. It was terrible, but she left it on the stereo anyway. It would be nice to have it playing when Rick came in.

Rick still hadn't arrived by the time the first side of the record was over. Lisa started to feel annoyed that she had rushed around, and now Rick was late. When the second side of the record was half over, Lisa began to wonder if Rick would show up at all. Then, just as the last song was beginning, the doorbell rang.

"Sorry I'm late," Rick apologized. "My friend was late dropping off the car."

"Oh, that's OK," said Lisa with a sweet smile. But to herself, she thought, "You could have called."

Lisa grabbed her jacket and they went out to the car. Well, it was at least part of a car. It was black, and it looked as if it hadn't had an easy life. The trunk lid was missing entirely, and the body was badly dented. Lisa let herself into the front seat while Rick got in on the driver's side. There were two other couples squeezed into the back. Lisa turned around to say hello.

Rick introduced everyone. "This is Lisa," he said to his friends. "And that's Danny and Beth and Allison and Scott." Lisa wasn't sure who belonged to which name, but she decided to figure it out later rather than to ask.

As soon as they entered the bowling alley, Lisa knew the evening was not going to go well. First of all, she had forgotten how noisy bowling alleys were. She had a hard time thinking with all that racket going on. Secondly, Lisa had forgotten about the special shoes people have to wear when they bowl. The others had brought their own shoes, but Lisa had to rent a pair. She hated the way they looked; but even more, she hated the fact that they smelled like old, unwashed socks.

The bowling itself turned out to be even worse than Lisa had feared. Allison went first. "She certainly looks like she knows what she's doing," thought Lisa. Allison scored seven on the first frame and looked disappointed. Danny got a strike.

"Lisa, you're next," said Beth, who was keeping score.

Lisa felt awkward and self-conscious. The ball weighed a ton. "If only they wouldn't watch me," she thought. "Well, here goes." She swung the enormous ball behind her. When she released it, it landed with a thud just a few feet in front of her. At the end of its long, slow journey down the alley, the ball managed—as if by accident—to knock down three pins.

"Not bad," said Rick. "On your next ball, try walking a few steps on the back-swing. Then bend your knee when you release the ball. And don't turn your wrist."

Lisa tried to follow Rick's instructions on her next turn, but nothing worked. The ball made a sharp turn to the left and went right into the gutter. When she turned around, she noticed that the others looked bored. She supposed they were wondering why Rick had brought her along.

Lisa was determined to do better on her next frame. She reviewed what Rick had told her and watched the others carefully. But when her turn came, she got another gutter ball. It seemed that the harder she tried, the worse she did.

Lisa couldn't tell what Rick was thinking. He wasn't being unpleasant, but he wasn't paying much attention to her, either. In fact, no one was paying much attention to her.

More and more, Lisa felt like an outsider. It depressed her to realize that she was waiting for the evening to end.

When they had finally bowled the last game, Lisa hoped they would drop the other couples off. Then she and Rick would have some time alone together. She might have a chance to save at least the end of the evening. But her heart sank when Scott said, "I'm starved. Let's get something to eat." It was decided that they would all go out for hamburgers.

Lisa felt so dismal that she didn't even perk up when Rick held her hand on the way to the car. Now she knew the evening would be a total failure.

Just as they reached the car, they heard a female voice calling, "Hey, Rick!" from across the parking lot. They turned around to see another couple walking toward them. Rick seemed glad to see them.

"Look who's here!" he said to the others. "It's Cheryl and Ken!"

"Where are you all going?" asked Cheryl.

"To get some burgers," Rick replied. "Want to come?"

Cheryl and Ken glanced at each other briefly, and then said, together, "Sure."

"OK, pile in!" said Rick cheerily.

This was too much for Lisa. She couldn't believe that Rick had asked two more people to join them. How would they all fit in the car?

"Uh . . . Rick," she said to him. "Could I talk to you for just a minute?" Then she drew him aside and whispered, "Don't you think the car will be too crowded with two more people?"

Rick looked at her as if he had no idea what she was talking about.

"I mean, it might be dangerous to have eight people in the car," Lisa continued.

From the look on Rick's face, she could see that she'd said the wrong thing.

"Look, Lisa," he said sharply, "I know what I'm doing. OK?"

Lisa could hear the anger in Rick's voice. It was obvious that he didn't want her advice. She decided to say no more. The evening had gone badly enough already. She'd only make it worse by having a fight with Rick in front of all these people.

"OK, Rick," she said softly. They walked over to the car, and Allison, Scott, Beth, and Danny climbed into their original seats in the back. Cheryl and Ken, determined to sit together, both piled into the front seat, next to Lisa. Ken sat next to Lisa, and then Cheryl sat in Ken's lap. Lisa was so jammed between them and Rick that she had to sit on the edge of the front seat. Her forehead almost touched the windshield.

Rick flipped on the radio. The rock music was so loud that they all had to scream to hear each other. "I hate this," thought Lisa. Ginny's words kept echoing in her mind: "What's so great about this guy, anyway?"

Then Lisa imagined herself ice-skating with Tom. She wondered if Tom had asked someone else to go skating with him to-night. Unexpectedly, Lisa felt a twinge of jealousy.

She stopped daydreaming as Rick pulled onto the highway. Traffic was heavy, and Rick wasn't concentrating on the road. Instead, he was alternately singing along with the radio and turning around to shout to the people in the backseat. Lisa wanted to ask him to watch what he was doing, but she was afraid to say anything after his reaction in the parking lot. She was feeling quite nervous when Beth leaned forward and yelled in Rick's ear, "Hey! This is the exit!"

Rick suddenly swerved into the right lane without signaling. Lisa looked back anxiously, terrified that another car might be coming up in that lane from behind them. To her horror, there *was* another car in the right lane. In a terrible fraction of a second, Lisa saw what was coming. She screamed, but it was too late.

The last things Lisa remembered were the sickening crash and the sharp blow of the windshield against her forehead.

When Lisa woke up, it was daylight. She could see that she was in a hospital room. She felt weak and had a throbbing pain in her head. When she moved, her head felt a lot worse.

Further exploration told her that there was a bandage on her forehead. Lying very still to keep the headache to a minimum, Lisa recalled the events of the previous evening. But the more she thought, the more questions crept into her mind.

What had happened to the other people in the car? Did anyone know where she was? How seriously was she hurt? In response to the last question, she tried moving her arms and legs. She was relieved to discover that they were working all right. Then she tested her memory. Since she knew her name, address, and telephone number, she decided that her brain was functioning.

Lisa's thoughts were interrupted when a woman in a white coat entered her room and walked over to Lisa's bed.

"Oh, good!" the woman said. "Glad to see you're awake. I'm Dr. Klein."

"Hello," Lisa said. "Yes, I'm awake. But I've got this awful headache."

"I don't doubt it," the doctor said. "Do you remember what happened to you?"

"I was in a car accident," Lisa replied. "Do you know what happened to the others?"

"You were the only one hurt badly enough to be kept here," Dr. Klein replied. "The others got patched up in the emergency room last night. But you're a lucky young woman, Lisa. You got away with a mild concussion and a few stitches. I'd like you to stay here for a few more days so we can keep an eye on you. After that, you should stay home for a good two weeks to rest."

"OK," Lisa said. "Dr. Klein, does anyone know I'm here? My roommate must be worried sick."

"Yes, the police notified your roommate last night," the doctor answered. "She's been here for hours, waiting for you to wake up. And there's a young man here to see you, too. I'll send them in now, but only for a few minutes." Then Dr. Klein wagged her finger at Lisa. "And you stay still."

The doctor turned and walked toward the door. Lisa couldn't help but wonder who the "young man" could be. Could it be Rick? It would be nice to know he cared enough to visit her.

A moment later, the door opened and Tom entered the room, followed by Ginny. They both rushed over to Lisa's bed.

"Hi, Lisa," Tom greeted her. He sounded cheerful, but he looked tired and worried.

Lisa was so glad to see him that she forgot to be disappointed that Rick hadn't come.

Ginny took Lisa's hand. "Boy, it's good to see you awake," Ginny said. "The police scared me to death last night. The car was totaled, you know."

"No great loss," Lisa said with a little smile.

"Lisa, how do you feel?" Tom asked. He was stroking her hair lightly, trying to avoid touching the bandage across her forehead.

"I have a headache," Lisa replied, "and I feel kind of weak. But I'm OK. The doctor said I'll have to stay here for a few more days. Then I'll have to rest at home for two weeks. I guess someone had better tell Van. I hope he'll be able to manage without me in the store."

"You just get well," said Tom, "and don't worry about the store."

Ginny reassured Lisa that Van would be able to get temporary help until Lisa went back to work. She also said that she had tried to reach Lisa's parents, but remembered that they were out of town. Lisa said she'd call them next week. They would just worry if they knew she'd been hurt.

The door opened, and a nurse poked her head inside the room.

"Sorry," the nurse said, "but visiting time is over now. Lisa should get some rest. You can come back this afternoon, if you'd like."

Suddenly, Lisa remembered that Tom was leaving for Florida today. She felt a wave of loneliness at the thought of him being so far away.

"Tom, have a good trip," she said, trying to sound cheerful. "Call when you get back."

Tom just smiled. "I'll see you this afternoon," he said. Then he leaned over and kissed Lisa lightly on the cheek.

Ginny squeezed Lisa's hand. "See you later," she said. "Get some rest."

After Tom and Ginny left the room, the nurse came in to check Lisa's pulse, temperature, and blood pressure. "Everything's fine," she said cheerfully. "Oh, and someone just left a message for you," she added. She pulled an envelope out of her pocket and handed it to Lisa.

Lisa tore open the envelope and glanced at the bottom of the note. It was from Rick. When she saw the writing, Lisa thought, "There are more words in this note than Rick has ever said to me out loud." Then she read the note.

Dear Lisa,

I'm really sorry about last night. You were right about overloading the car. I feel

*terrible about the accident, and I don't
know what to say to you—except to tell you
again how sorry I am.*

*I stopped by to visit you this morning,
but the nurse said you had visitors. Also, to
tell you the truth, I was afraid you'd be
angry. I wouldn't blame you if you were!*

*Anyway, I hope you feel better soon. If
you want to talk to me, give me a call. My
home number is 340-0613.*

Love, Rick

Lisa folded the note and slipped it under
her pillow. From his words, it was clear
that Rick really did like her. But maybe he
was just one of those guys who didn't know
how to express his feelings in person.

Lisa wasn't sure how she felt about Rick
anymore. But she did know that she

wasn't angry, and she didn't want him to feel guilty about the accident. In fact, she even felt sorry for him.

Suddenly, Lisa felt very tired. As she let herself drift into sleep, she happily remembered Tom's words. "I'll see you this afternoon," he'd said. Had he postponed his trip?

When Lisa awoke for the second time that day, it was late afternoon. She lay with her eyes closed, noticing that she still felt weak. But the pain in her head had diminished to a dull ache.

Although her eyes were closed, Lisa sensed someone's presence in the room. She opened her eyes to see Tom standing at the foot of her bed. Behind him, on a table, was a vase of lovely flowers.

"Hi," she said to him. "The flowers are beautiful."

"So are you," Tom answered with a sweet smile. "Even with that bandage on your head. How's the headache?"

"Much better, thanks," Lisa replied.

"I'm glad," Tom said. "I was really scared when Ginny called last night. Lisa, if anything happened to you, I don't know what I'd do."

"Oh, Tom," Lisa said, "it means a lot to me to know how much you care." Then, because she meant it, she added, "I'd feel the same way if anything happened to you."

Tom moved over to the chair at the side of the bed. He sat down, taking Lisa's hand in his.

"Tom," Lisa said, "aren't you going to Florida?"

"I've postponed my trip for a while," Tom said. "My brother said I can come another time."

"I'm really sorry about ruining your vacation," Lisa said apologetically. But then she confessed, "But I'm glad you'll be around."

Tom glanced down at Lisa's hand and then looked back into her eyes. "Listen," he said softly. "Do you feel well enough to answer a tough question?"

"Well, ask away," Lisa said with a smile. "Then I'll see if I can answer the question."

Tom swallowed and then began to speak. "Well, I know we've been best friends since we were kids," he said. "When we were dating in high school, we were just too young to be serious." Then he paused. After a moment, he went on.

"Now, here's the question. Do you think we could try again? I mean, try being more than just friends? I . . . I've never met a woman I liked as much as I like you, Lisa."

Lisa didn't know what to say. Since this morning, her feelings for Tom had seemed to grow stronger. On the other hand, the note from Rick was still under her pillow.

Finally, Lisa spoke. "I care about you a lot too, Tom," she said, squeezing his hand. "But I need a little time to think before I answer that question. Could you wait awhile for my answer?"

"Sure," Tom said with a smile. "No problem. I don't want to pressure you into anything. No matter what, our friendship will always be important to me."

Before Tom left, he leaned over Lisa's bed and kissed her lips very gently and tenderly. It was definitely not a "just friends" kind of kiss. Lisa could feel her heart pounding as Tom pulled away.

Tom left, and Lisa lay there for a moment in a state of confusion. Then she pulled Rick's note from under her pillow and read it again. When she had decided what to say to him, she dialed his number.

"Hi, Rick," she said when he answered. "It's Lisa."

"Oh, wow!" Rick exclaimed. "Am I glad to hear your voice! I was sure you'd never speak to me again. How are you?"

Lisa assured Rick that she was all right. Then he continued.

"I really acted like a jerk last night," he said. "In fact, I've been rotten to you ever since our first date. I guess I just didn't know a good thing when I saw it. What I'm trying to say is that if you're not too mad at me, I'd like another chance."

"I'm not mad," Lisa replied. "And thank you for the note. It was really sweet, and it made me feel much better."

"Could I stop by tomorrow to visit you?" Rick asked.

Lisa didn't think it would be the greatest idea to have Rick and Tom meet in her hospital room. Besides, as she had told Tom, she needed some time to think things through.

"Would you mind waiting until I got home?" she answered.

"Not at all," said Rick. "Just call when you're ready. I've got patience."

As she hung up, Lisa realized that she was in a position many women would envy. Two very cute guys were falling in love with her. But she was too confused to enjoy it.

On Monday, Valentine's Day, Lisa went home from the hospital. That evening, she sat in her favorite armchair and stared at the two Valentine cards in her lap. One was from Rick, and the other from Tom.

"Well, aren't you the popular one?" said Ginny with a smile.

Lisa looked up at Ginny with a miserable expression on her face. "Oh, Ginny," she said. "I know a lot of women would give anything to have this problem. But I'd give anything *not* to have it! I just don't know what to do!"

"Well, I'm not supposed to tell you this," Ginny said, "but I'm going to, anyway. Tom went by Van's Saturday morning to tell him about your accident. He told Van to call him if he couldn't find a temporary replacement for you. Well, Van called Tom Sunday morning. He couldn't find anyone to cover for you, and he was going crazy in the store with no help. So Tom is using his vacation time to work in the shop until you get back to work."

"Oh, no!" Lisa exclaimed. "He gave up his vacation to do that?"

"He sure did," Ginny replied.

Lisa sat quietly for a moment. Then she said, "You know, he's really something!"

"I agree," Ginny said. "But that's just *my* opinion." Then she disappeared into the kitchen.

Even though Ginny was out of sight, Lisa continued. "I've been doing some thinking for the last few days. Rick may be a nice guy, and he's certainly handsome. But we have nothing at all in common. I keep wishing we could have fun together and understand each other better, but it doesn't happen. And Tom and I have so much in common! I don't know why I didn't see it long ago."

"Well, I won't say, 'I told you so'!" Ginny called from the kitchen. "What are you going to do about Rick?"

"I'd better call him," sighed Lisa.

As she dialed Rick's number, Lisa felt nervous. She wanted to get her point across without hurting his feelings.

When he answered, Lisa first thanked Rick for the valentine. Then, before he had a chance to reply, she launched into her speech. "Rick, I want you to understand that I'm not angry with you. In fact, I like you a lot. But I have to confess something. I wanted to go out with you so badly that I pretended to like the things you like. Actually, I hate horror movies, I despise Lowlife, and I *abhor* bowling. We have so little in common that I don't see how we could get along. I think you're nice, but I don't think you're for me."

Then she stopped. "There! I've said it!" she thought to herself.

"I hate to say it," Rick sighed, "but I think you've got a point."

"You do?" Lisa asked with surprise. She had expected an argument.

Rick continued. "I have something to confess, too," he said. "I have this problem. I seem to like only women who play hard to get. I could tell that you really liked me, so

I didn't try very hard to be nice to you. I guess that sounds crazy, but that's the way I am."

Lisa laughed. "Well, since we're being honest with each other, it does sound a little crazy."

"Anyway," Rick said, "I think I've learned a lesson. I should really thank you. Next time a great woman like you comes along, maybe I won't mess up again."

They chatted comfortably for a few more minutes and then hung up. After she put the receiver down, Lisa called to Ginny, "It's safe to come out of the kitchen now!"

Ginny popped out of the kitchen with, "How did it go?"

"Fine," answered Lisa. "Now I can't wait to see Tom. He's coming over in half an hour."

"I'll call Peter and we'll go to a movie," Ginny said. "I don't want to spend the whole night in the kitchen."

A half hour later, Tom stood in the doorway. He held a heart-shaped box of candy in one hand and a long-stemmed pink rose in the other.

"Oh, Tom," Lisa whispered to him. "You're wonderful!" Her eyes sparkled as she put her arms around him.

Tom hugged her back as best he could. Then he said, "What did I do to deserve this?"

With her arms still around him, Lisa said, "Don't be mad at Ginny, but she told me what you've been up to. Why didn't you tell me?"

"Could I put these things down and come in?" Tom said with a laugh. "Then

I'll explain." Lisa had always liked Tom's open smile and easy laugh. Now they seemed especially wonderful to her.

They sat down on the sofa, holding hands. "I didn't want you to know just yet," Tom explained, "because I didn't take the job just so you'd like me better. I took it because . . . because I love you, Lisa."

"Oh, Tom," Lisa said with tears in her eyes. "You're so good to me!"

Tom looked deeply into Lisa's eyes. "Do you really think you could fall in love with me? After all these years of being 'just friends'?"

"I already have," Lisa replied. "But you have to promise me one thing."

"Anything," Tom answered.

"Will you always be my best friend?" Lisa asked.

"Of course," Tom said as he pulled Lisa toward him. "After all, that's the best kind of love."